The Little Green Island
With a Little Red House

A Book of Colors and Critters

by Sharon Lovejoy

Down East Books

ISBN: 0-89272-673-3
LCCN: 2004117292
Printed In China   FCI

2   4   5   3   1

Down East Books
A division of Down East Enterprise, Inc.,
Publisher of *Down East*, the Magazine of Maine

Book orders: 1-800-685-7962
www.downeastbooks.com

For my favorite
little nature lovers...

Sara May Arnold

Evan & Tessa Borchardt

Anna & Kara Brewer

Erika Mathieson

Sammy Rae Means

Asher Prostovich

Ilyahna Prostovich

Sydney Watt

On a little green

island

stands a little red

house

with a little orange

cat

a little gray

mouse

a little rose

moth

a little beige

bat

who sleeps
upside-down

on a little

hat rack

And beneath the shaggy
edge of a little purple

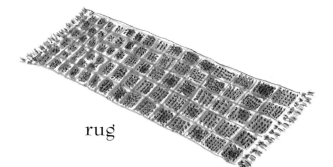

rug

it has a roly-poly
polka-dotty

little copper

bug

The little green

island

has a little chartreuse

frog

who searches for his
supper on a little mossy

log

It has a leafy little peach

tree

a little mocha

mole

a little ochre

cricket

who peeks out

from a hole

It has a little patch
of violets

in a shady little glen

and a little
russet

fox

with three

kits

inside her den

The little green

island

has a little lilac

shell

and a little cobalt

bird

with a voice
just like a

bell

It has a

little olive

snail

with a

little slimy

tail

who slithers
through the

forest

on a
slippery, shiny trail

The little green

island

has a little khaki

toad

a little yellow-sided

snake

who basks along
the road

It has a little azure

butterfly

and a little little white-striped

skunk

who spends
all her days
in a little plum

tree's

trunk

The little green

island

has a little scarlet

newt

who lives all alone
in a little rubber

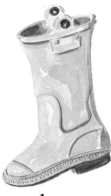

boot

It has a little chestnut

chipmunk

and a little

saffron

spider

who bundles
up her little

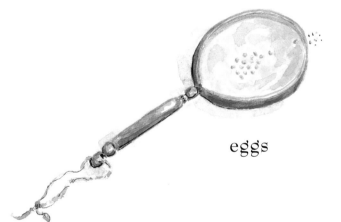

eggs

and keeps them
close beside her

The little green

island

has a little black-rumped

bee

a little pink-tongued

porcupine

who hangs

out in a

tree

And in a little silver

tide pool

by the sparkling
sapphire

sea

the little green

island

has a someone
just like me!

Faretheewell

Dear Reader,
And now it's
time to stop
&
Look — for
colors found
outside your
book!
Sharon Lovejoy